BIRTHDAY BOOK

donated to the elementary School
Library Media Center
in honor of

birthday,

Clever Cat

PETER COLLINGTON

Alfred A. Knopf · New York

THIS IS A BORZOI BOOK PUBLISHED BY ALFRED A. KNOPF, INC.

Copyright © 2000 by Peter Collington

All rights reserved under International and Pan-American Copyright Conventions.
Published in the United States by Alfred A. Knopf, Inc., New York, and simultaneously in
Canada by Random House of Canada Limited, Toronto. Distributed by Random House, Inc., New York.
Published in Great Britain in 2000 by Jonathan Cape Limited. First American edition, 2000.

KNOPF, BORZOI BOOKS, and the colophon are registered trademarks of Random House, Inc.

www.randomhouse.com/kids

Library of Congress Cataloging-in-Publication Data
Collington, Peter.
Clever cat / by Peter Collington.
p.   cm.
Summary: When Mr. and Mrs. Ford discover that Tibs the cat can get his own food, they give him a house key and a credit card,
but when they make him get a job, do the shopping, and pay the rent, he begins to wonder if he is really that clever after all.
ISBN 0-375-80477-3 (trade). — ISBN 0-375-90477-8 (lib. bdg.)
[1. Cats—Fiction.] I. Title.
PZ7.C686Cl   2000
[E]—dc21   98-40373

Printed in Singapore
August 2000
10 9 8 7 6 5 4 3 2 1

Every morning Tibs waited by his front door.

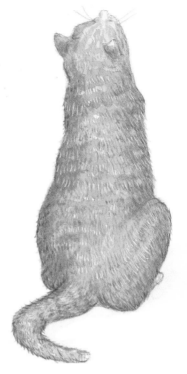

And waited...

And waited...

And waited...

And waited...

And waited... And waited...

Until someone noticed him.

"I suppose you want your breakfast," said Mrs. Ford, his owner.

"Well, you're just going to have to wait."

"Get out of my way, CAT!" shouted Mr. Ford. "I'm late for work."

"Not now," said Miss Ford. "I'm late for school."

"MOVE, STUPID!" said Master Ford.

Tibs waited...   And waited...

And waited, until Mrs. Ford noticed him again. "Why can't you feed yourself, you great fat lump? You always make me late."

Finally, Tibs had his breakfast.

And so it went, day in and day out. Waiting for breakfast; waiting for lunch; waiting for dinner.

One morning Tibs could take it no longer.
He climbed up to the cupboard and got down his own cat food.

He opened the can, served himself a generous portion, and started to eat.

The house went very quiet. No one was rushing. Everyone was looking at him.

"What a clever cat," said Mrs. Ford. "I had no idea."

"Amazing," said Mr. Ford.

"Wow!" said Miss and Master Ford.

The next day Mrs. Ford gave Tibs his own front door key.
"Try it out," she said. He did.
"What a clever cat," said Mrs. Ford, rushing off to work.

The day after that Mrs. Ford gave Tibs her cash card.
"I forgot to pick you up some cat food," she said. "Do you think you
can take out some cash and buy yourself some dinner?"
Tibs nodded. "Clever cat," said Mrs. Ford. "Must rush."

Tibs drew some cash...

and bought two cans of cat food.

The neighbors were impressed. "I wish we had a clever cat who could do its own shopping," they said, looking down at their lazy kitties snoozing in the sun.

The lazy kitties opened their eyes for a moment and winked at each other. Then they went back to snoozing.

Tibs tried snoozing himself, but he was restless and couldn't.

He went out for a stroll. It was lunchtime and Tibs was feeling hungry.

He got out some cash from the machine and went into a café.

What fine food! How awful cat food tasted in comparison.
However had he put up with it all these years?

Tibs left a big tip for the waitress. The café manager gave him a wave
as he left. The customers smiled at him.

The next day Tibs went shopping...

and then went to a movie.

Every day there was something different to do and new friends to make.

How much fun life could be. Snoozing in the day was for dumb cats!
What a waste of time.

Tibs was just on his way out to have breakfast at his favorite café
when Mr. and Mrs. Ford stopped him.
Mrs. Ford snatched back her cash card.

"We need to talk," said Mr. Ford. "You're a very clever cat, but a very expensive one to keep. You're going to have to help out with the bills."

"We need rent money from you, also," added Mrs. Ford.

"I think you need to find a job."

Tibs went to see the manager at his favorite café about a job.
"Okay," said the manager. "I'll try you out as a waiter."

Tibs worked all day.
Carrying this...

Carrying that...   Never any rest...

By the end of the day Tibs was exhausted.

He still had his own meal to make at home and his dishes
to wash up afterward.

And when Tibs got paid at the end of the week, most of his money went to bills and rent.

He only had enough left over to buy himself cat food.

Tibs was so tired on Monday morning that he failed to get up.

When he arrived at work late, the manager took him aside.
"I've had a lot of complaints about you from customers," he said.
"You make people wait too long for their meals. Sorry, but I have to let you go."

When Mr. and Mrs. Ford learned that Tibs didn't have a job anymore,
they were not very sympathetic. "You better find another job quick,"
said Mr. Ford. "We need your money coming in."

Tibs went outside. All the other cats were happily snoozing without a care in the world.

The next morning Tibs waited by the front door.

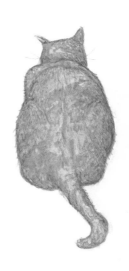

And waited...   And waited...   And waited...

"Where's your key?" said Mrs. Ford. Tibs looked blank.

And then he waited... And waited... And waited for breakfast.

"Forgotten how to feed yourself, I suppose?" said Mrs. Ford.
"Well, don't expect me to help you." Tibs looked blank.

Then he waited...

And waited...

And waited...

He didn't mind.

Finally, the next day, Mrs. Ford broke down and fed Tibs herself.
"Dumb cat," she said, rushing off to work.

Tibs found a nice sunny spot outside and curled up and began
to snooze.
The other cats on the street opened their eyes for a moment
and winked at each other as if to say, "Finally, a clever cat."